# Tom and Ricky

## and the

# Video Game Spy

**Bob Wright**

**High Noon Books**
Novato, California

**Cover Design: Nancy Peach**
**Interior Illustrations: Herb Heidinger**

International Standard Book Number: 0-87879-331-3

9 8 7 6 5 4 3
25 24 23 22 21

You'll enjoy all the High Noon Books. Write for a free full list of titles.

# Contents

# CHAPTER 1

## Nothing To Do

Ricky could hear the phone. His mother was at the store. His dad was working on the car.

"Ricky, will you get it? I'm busy with the car," his dad called out.

Ricky picked up the phone. "Hello," he said.

"Ricky, this is Tom. What are you doing today?" Tom asked.

"Not much. How about you?" Ricky asked.

"Want to go to the video store?" Tom asked.

"Sure. They have a new game," Ricky said.

"That's the one I want to see," Tom said.

"I do, too. It's a new star game. Everyone says it's a good one," Ricky said.

"I'll see you there. Can you be there in 15 minutes?" Tom asked.

"OK," Ricky said. "I have to tell my dad where I'm going."

Ricky put the phone down. "Dad, I'm going to meet Tom. We're going to West's Video Store."

"Wait a minute. I can't hear you," his dad called out.

Ricky's dad came into the house. "Where are you going?" he asked.

"Tom and I are going to West's Video Store," Ricky said.

2

"What are you going to do there?" his dad asked.

"Tom and I are going to see the new video game," Ricky said.

"Don't get in Mr. West's way. That is a busy store," his dad said.

"Mr. West is nice. He lets us play the games," Ricky said.

"Yes, Mr. West has been nice. But don't get in his way. Don't stay too long," his dad said.

"I won't. I'll be back soon," Ricky called.

"I want you to help me today," his dad said.

"OK. We won't stay too long," Ricky said.

Patches saw Ricky going out of the house. He wanted to go, too. He started to bark.

"You can't go, Patches. They won't let you in the store. You stay here," Ricky said.

Patches looked back at Ricky. Then he went and sat down.

Ricky got on his bike. He was on his way to West's Video Store. He wanted to get there first. Tom didn't have as far to go. Ricky went as fast as he could.

## CHAPTER 2

## The Video Store

Tom got to the store first. Then Ricky got there. Ricky stopped his bike. They both locked their bikes. Then they went into the store.

There were a lot of people in the store. They were all looking at the video games. They wanted to buy them. Most of the people were playing the new star game. There was a long line for each game.

"Look at all the people," Tom said.

"There sure are a lot of them," Ricky said.

They saw Bill. He worked for Mr. West. Bill looked very busy.

"Hi, Bill," Ricky called out. Bill saw them. He walked over to them.

"I bet you want to play the new game," he said.

"We sure do," Ricky said.

"I have to go now. There is a lot to do today," Bill said. Then he left.

They looked as people kept playing the games. Then, all of a sudden, one game had no people. They ran over to it. They played it.

After a while Mr. West came over to them.

"I can't let you boys play at this any longer. There are other people who want to see the new game," he said.

The games were free. The people didn't want to go. Mr. West had to let them know they couldn't stay too long at each game.

Tom and Ricky walked around the store. There were lots of things to see.

Then they saw a man talking to Mr. West.

"I got this game last week. It doesn't work. I want my money back," the man said.

"We cannot give you your money back. We will give you a game that works," Mr. West said. He took the game from the man and gave him another one.

Mr. West took the game to Bill. "Bill, will you see if this game works? That man who just left said it didn't."

7

Bill took the game into the back room. He tried the game. He wasn't gone too long. Then he went back to Mr. West.

*"I got this game last week. It doesn't work. I want my money back," the man said.*

"Mr. West, this game works," he said.

"Well, we can't sell it now as a new game. It is used," Mr. West said.

Tom could hear Mr. West talking. "How much do you want for it?" Tom asked.

"Do you want to buy it?" Mr. West asked.

"Yes, I would," Tom said.

"Well, let's see. It was $20.00 new. I can sell it for $10.00," Mr. West said.

Tom turned to Ricky and said, "Ricky, we can buy that game for $10.00!"

"Tom, do you have $10.00?" Ricky asked.

"Well, no, I don't. Can we buy it together?" Tom said.

Mr. West saw Tom and Ricky talking.

"Why don't you boys think about it? Then let me know. I will keep the game for one hour. Then I will have to sell it to someone else," Mr. West said.

Tom and Ricky walked out of the store.

Ricky said to Tom, "Where are we going to get $10.00?"

"I have some money from my birthday," Tom said.

"Wait. I have some money from helping Mrs. Jones clean her yard," Ricky said.

They got on their bikes. Then Ricky said, "Tom, wait. Where are we going to play the game?"

"We can play it at Eddie's house," Tom said.

"OK. I'll be back here in 30 minutes. See you then," Ricky said.

Then they both left.

# CHAPTER 3

## At Eddie's House

When Ricky got back to the store, Tom was there. They each had $5.00. They went into the store to see Mr. West.

There were still many people in the store.

They saw Mr. West. He was talking to people. Many people were buying video games.

"Mr. West, we have the money for the star game," Tom said.

Mr. West looked at Tom. He said, "You boys wanted to buy that game. Just a minute."

Mr. West left and then came back. He had the game for them.

Tom and Ricky each gave him $5.00.

"That's right. This game is $10.00 because it is used. Have fun with it," Mr. West said.

Tom and Ricky got on their bikes. They left for Eddie's house.

When they got there, Eddie was playing another game on his set.

"Look what we have," Ricky said.

Eddie liked to play video games. He had a lot of them, but he didn't have the new one.

"That's the new star game," Eddie said.

"We just got it. Mr. West let us have it for $10.00," Tom said.

"We were lucky to get it," Ricky said.

"How come?" Eddie asked.

"A man was mad. He said it didn't work right. But Mr. West played it and said it was OK," Tom said.

Eddie put the game into his set. They all got ready to play it.

Eddie looked at the game. So did Tom and Ricky. Then Eddie said, "This is not right. The star ships should be red. Those are blue."

Eddie had played the game at Mr. West's store. So had Tom and Ricky.

"Maybe this is the bad one. Maybe that man was right. Do you think Mr. West got the games mixed up?" Ricky asked.

They tried to play some more. The colors were all mixed up.

"Let's go and see Mr. West," Ricky said.

*Eddie looked at the game. "This is not right. The star ships should be red."*

"Come on, Eddie. You come, too," Tom said.

They all got on their bikes.

The store was full of people.

Mr. West saw Tom, Ricky, and Eddie. "How's everything? Do you like the game?" he said to them.

"We like the game, Mr. West. But it isn't right," Tom said.

"That's funny. I looked at it myself and it was OK," Mr. West said.

"The colors aren't right," Ricky said.

Then Eddie said, "My set is OK, Mr. West. All the other games I have are fine. This one has the colors all mixed up."

"Let me try it out again," Mr. West said.

Then Tom saw the man who had the game the first time. He was back in the store.

"Look. There's the man who had the game the first time," Tom said. "He is talking to Bill."

# CHAPTER 4

## The Man Comes Back

Bill and the man were talking. The man looked mad. No one could hear what they were saying. There were too many people in the store.

Bill was not talking. The man was doing all the talking. Bill saw Mr. West looking at them. He told the man. The man went over to Mr. West. He was mad but he tried to look nice.

"I'm Mr. Bush," the man said.

"Yes, you were in the store this morning," Mr. West said.

"The new star video game doesn't work right either," Mr. Bush said.

Mr. West called Bill over. "Bill, Mr. Bush says he got another video game that is not right. What is going on?"

Bill looked at Mr. West. Then he looked at Mr. Bush. "I don't know, Mr. West."

"We have one that isn't right," Tom said.

"What do you mean?" Mr. Bush said.

"The colors are all mixed up," Ricky said.

Mr. West saw some people who needed help. "Wait. I will be right back," he said.

Mr. Bush said, "Tell me about your game."

"It is all mixed up. I know that game. I played it here in Mr. West's store," Eddie said.

Then Mr. West called Bill. "Bill, come over here. I need your help." Mr. West looked very busy. Bill went over to him.

"Boys, the colors on my game are OK. Why don't you give me that one, and I'll give you this one," Mr. Bush said.

"But you said yours wasn't right," Tom said.

"I think I don't know how to play the game," Mr. Bush said.

"Are the colors on your game all right?" Eddie asked.

"Yes, they are fine," Mr. Bush said.

Tom looked at Ricky. "Let's do it."

"But why do you want our game? It isn't right," Ricky said.

"It will be fun for me. Maybe I can fix it," Mr. Bush said.

Mr. West came back. "Bill will be here in a minute. I'm sorry I had to leave."

"Everything is fine, Mr. West," Eddie said.

"Mr. Bush is going to give us his game. We will give him this one," Ricky said.

"Wait a minute. Mr. Bush, you said the game wasn't right. Now you want their game. It has the colors all mixed up," Mr. West said.

"I'm sorry about all of this," Mr. Bush said. "I just want the boys to have a good game. I'll take the one that isn't right."

"Wait. Let me talk with Bill," Mr. West said. "Bill, come here. I want to talk to you."

Bill looked at Mr. West. He could tell that something was wrong. He saw that Mr. Bush was with Tom, Ricky, and Eddie.

# CHAPTER 5

## Something Is Wrong

Mr. West and Bill walked into the back room.

Mr. West said, "Bill, what is going on?"

"What do you mean?" Bill asked.

"Mr. Bush got the star game. Then he came back. We gave him another one. Now he is back again. Then the boys came back and their game is wrong," Mr. West said.

"Maybe lots of the games are wrong," Bill said.

"Now, Bill, that's silly," Mr. West said.

Mr. West was not smiling. He looked upset.

"What do you think we should do?" Bill

asked.

*Mr. West and Bill walked into the back room.*
*Mr. West said, "Bill, what is going on?"*

"Mr. Bush wants to give his game to the boys. He wants their game. But the boys said their game is not right," Mr. West said.

"Let Mr. Bush take their game," Bill said.

"No. I want to see those games myself. I will look at them tonight," Mr. West said.

Mr. West and Bill went back into the store.

"We want to see the games. Can you come back tomorrow?" Mr. West said.

"But the boys are going to give me their game. I will give them mine," Mr. Bush said.

"No. I want to find out what is wrong," Mr. West said.

"We can come back," Eddie said.

Mr. Bush looked mad. He looked very mad.

Mr. Bush looked at Bill for a long time.

"All right. I will be back tomorrow," Mr. Bush said. Then he left.

"Bill, Mr. Bush has been here many times. Do you know him very well?" Mr. West said.

"Well . . . I . . . I . . . ," Bill said.

"Bill, I can't hear you," Mr. West said.

"I sell him games when he comes in. He always comes to me," Bill said.

"Have any games been wrong?" Mr. West asked.

"No. This is the first time he has come back," Bill said.

"I need to check those games myself," Mr. West said.

Bill looked funny. "Is something wrong, Bill?" Mr. West asked.

"No. No. Everything is fine," Bill said.

**CHAPTER 6**

## The Next Day

That night Mr. West got a lot of games out. He wanted to find out what was wrong. Something had to be wrong. The video game factory never sent him games that were wrong.

He played Mr. Bush's game. It was all right.

Then he played Tom and Ricky's game. The colors were not right. He looked at the box the game came in. The box looked funny to him. It was not like the other boxes for the new star game.

The next day Mr. West said, "Bill, something is wrong. Mr. Bush's game is all right. But Tom and Ricky's game is wrong."

Bill didn't say anything.

"Look at the box that Tom and Ricky's game came in," Mr. West said.

Bill looked at the box. Then he said, "I don't see anything wrong with it."

"The star ships on all the boxes are red. On this one box they are green," Mr. West said.

"That's right. This one is not like the other boxes," Bill said.

"Let's see if any other boxes are wrong," Mr. West said.

They looked at all of the boxes in the store.

That was the only one that was wrong.

"This is funny. The game is not right. The box is not right," Mr. West said.

Bill didn't say anything. Mr. West didn't say anything.

"What are you thinking, Mr. West?" Bill said.

"I think something is funny about all of this. I want to talk with Mr. Bush when he comes to the store today," Mr. West said.

"I'll tell you when he comes in," Bill said.

"Come on. People are coming into the store," Mr. West said.

Many people were coming in. One was a policeman. He was with his son. "We want to buy the new star game," the policeman said.

Tom and Ricky walked into the store. "Let's wait here for Eddie," Ricky said.

"He should be here soon," Tom said.

*One man was a policeman. He was with his son.*

Then Mr. Bush came in. He saw Tom and Ricky. "Where's your friend?" he asked.

"He said he'd be here," Tom said.

Then Eddie got there on his bike. He said, "Let's go see Mr. West and get our games."

They all walked into the store. Bill saw them walk in. He was with some people. He couldn't go to talk with them. Mr. West saw them. He walked over to talk to them. By this time there were many people in the store.

"I think I know why that one game was wrong," Mr. West said.

Just then the policeman walked over to Mr. West. He wanted to ask about the new star game.

Mr. Bush saw the policeman coming.

Mr. Bush started to run out of the store. He pushed people. They fell down. The policeman knew something was wrong. He ran to get Mr. Bush. He grabbed him and they went back into the store.

# CHAPTER 7

## Bill Talks

Mr. West looked at Mr. Bush. Bill came over to see what was wrong. The policeman was holding Mr. Bush.

"Let's all go in the back," Mr. West said.

They all went with Mr. West.

The policeman said, "What's going on? Why did you run out of the store?"

Mr. Bush didn't say anything.

Mr. West looked at Bill. "Bill, you know something."

Mr. Bush still didn't say anything.

Bill didn't say anything. He just looked at Mr. West and then at Mr. Bush.

Then Mr. West said, "There is something funny about some of the games. I think that each big box of games we get has one game that is wrong."

"What do you mean?" the policeman asked.

"I am not sure. But I think Mr. Bush wants the games that are wrong," Mr. West said.

The policeman looked at Bill. "Do you know Mr. Bush?" he asked.

"I have seen him in the store," Bill said.

"Bill helps Mr. Bush get games," Mr. West said.

"What do you have to say?" the policeman said to Mr. Bush.

"I'm not saying anything," Mr. Bush said.

"Well, then I will have to take you in," the policeman said.

All of a sudden Bill yelled, "Wait. I'll talk. I don't know how I got into this. I'll talk."

"What do you want to say?" the policeman said to Bill.

"I got money for giving Mr. Bush the video games in the wrong boxes," Bill said.

"Who gave you money?" Mr. West asked.

"Mr. Bush did. When he came in, he wanted the box with the wrong colors," Bill said. "He always gave me $50.00 for that box."

"Don't say anything," Mr. Bush yelled.

"Keep on talking," the policeman said.

"The colors on the wrong game mean something. I don't know what they mean. Mr. Bush is a . . . a . . . a spy," Bill said.

"Bill, what are you saying?" Mr. West asked.

"I'm very sorry," Bill said. "I did all of this for the money. Now I am sorry."

"I'll get you for this," Mr. Bush said to Bill.

"Go on," the policeman said.

"Someone at the factory made one wrong game. That game was sent to this store," Bill said.

"I'm taking both of you in. I'll need those games, Mr. West," the policeman said.

"It's OK with me. Take what you need,"
Mr. West said.

Bill looked at Mr. West. "I'm sorry," he said.

*"Mr. Bush is a . . . a . . . a spy," Bill said.*

"Bill, you helped a spy. That was wrong,"
Mr. West said.

The policeman took Mr. Bush and Bill to
his car.

# CHAPTER 8

## The Spy

The next day Tom and Ricky went back to the video store. Mr. West saw them.

"Mr. Bush told the police everything," Mr. West said.

"What was this all about?" Ricky asked.

"Someone at the video factory made one wrong game. That game was sent to my store. Bill had to get the wrong game and keep it. When Mr. Bush came in, he gave him that game," Mr. West said.

"What about the wrong colors on the game?" Tom asked.

"Each wrong color means something. When Mr. Bush saw a wrong color, it told him to do something," Mr. West said.

"But why did Mr. Bush need to get the game with the wrong colors?" Ricky asked.

"Mr. Bush is a spy. He works for another video factory. Someone at the star video game factory was telling Mr. Bush about new games. Then Mr. Bush told his factory about the new games," Mr. West said.

"I don't get it," Tom said.

"Tom, it takes a long time to make a video game," Mr. West said.

"Now I see. Mr. Bush's factory could come out first with a new game," Ricky said.

"That's right," Mr. West said. "I called the star game factory. They got the man who made the wrong game that was sent here."

"What about Bill? I liked him," Ricky said.

"Mr. Bush gave him money. Bill got a lot of money when he gave Mr. Bush the wrong game. Bill wanted to stop doing this a long time ago. Mr. Bush told him he could not stop. He had to keep on doing it," Mr. West said.

"I hope he will be all right," Tom said.

"I do, too," Mr. West said.

"Wait. I need to give you a game," Mr. West said.

"That's right," Tom said.

"Here, take this one. I know it is all right," Mr. West said.

Tom and Ricky took the game and went to their bikes.

"I hope this one works all right," Tom said.

"This time I don't care if the colors are wrong. I just want to play the game," Ricky said.

"Come back again," Mr. West called.

"We sure will," Ricky called back.